THESE SEAS COUNT!

Alison Formento   Illustrated by **Sarah Snow**

Albert Whitman & Company
Chicago, Illinois

Something happened to Sunnyside Beach. Something bad. So on Beach Clean-Up Day, Mr. Tate's class wanted to help. When they arrived at the seashore, they met Captain Ned.

"Yo-ho! That's my boat, the *Sea Fan*. I do my best to care for the oceans and seas, but I need some help today."

The class walked with Captain Ned along the shore. They saw dirty bottles and cans, empty food containers, plastic bags, and even old tires. Gulls stood among piles of trash.

"The sea is sad," said Captain Ned. He waved his hat out wide. "This garbage worries it."

"Seas can't be sad," Eli said.

Captain Ned put on his hat. "Listen closely, and the sea will share a story."

Everyone stood at the surf's edge. Waves lapped at their feet, and a breeze blew salty air. This is what they heard . . .

One whale leaps high, breaching my surface.

TWO giant sea turtles surf through a seaweed forest.

Three mighty marlins glide across my waves.

Four sea horses gallop in a saltwater rodeo.

Five flapping rays skim above my sandy floor.

"I wish I could swim like that," said Jake.

"Sshh!" said Shin. "The sea has more to say."

A wave crashed on the beach.

Six pelicans slurp fish, filling their empty pouches.

Seven *jellyfish drift by, dancing a water ballet.*

Eight gulls plunge and dip
before soaring high.

Nine harbor seals sprawl on boulders, resting after a swim.

Ten bottlenose dolphins dive and leap, flying through the air.

Over and under my waves, I am a home for many—
from the deepest deep to beaches, sandy dunes, and sky.

"What do you hear?" asked Captain Ned.

"This sea counts!" Shin said.

"What else is great about the sea?" asked Mr. Tate.

"Good food!" said Jake. "I love to eat fish."

"The oceans and seas feed people all over the world," said Captain Ned. "They also feed fish. In every bucket of ocean water, there are millions of tiny plants called *phytoplankton*. These plants are food for small fish, which become food for bigger fish. When seawater is polluted, phytoplankton can't grow."

Mr. Tate said, "If the oceans and seas aren't clean, that hurts fish *and* people."

"Beaches are fun," said Natalie. "But it's so dirty here."

Captain Ned held up a plastic bottle. "Trash comes from boats or from land, where it's washed into the sea by rivers and streams. Sometimes accidents happen, and oil, sewage, or dangerous chemicals pollute seawater. This harms sea creatures and ruins our beaches, too."

A sand crab limped by with a plastic bag trailing from its leg. Eli ran after the crab to help. "Oof!"

Jake helped Eli.

"It's smelly here!" Jake said.

Amy found a dead starfish in a pool of murky water. "I feel bad for all the fish in the sea."

"I do, too," said Mr. Tate. "That's why we need to keep our world's water clean."

Mr. Tate pointed to a cloud over the ocean. "Remember when we studied the water cycle? We saw how oceans and seas help create weather."

"We learned a poem about that," said Eli. He held his arms in a big circle.
   "Ocean waves evaporate.
      Cloudy skies condensate.
         Rain and snow come down.
            Water goes round and round!"

"Yo-ho!" said Captain Ned. "The oceans help keep our air clean, too."

"How?" asked Natalie.

"Phytoplankton create oxygen like plants do. And they absorb dirty air made when we use coal, oil, and gasoline." Captain Ned took a deep breath.

A wind gusted up, and the gulls that were perched on the trash flew out over the water.

"Seas sure can do a lot," Shin said.

Captain Ned nodded. Everyone helped clean Sunnyside Beach.
They picked up. They carted. They carried.

Mr. Tate's class filled
one, two, three,
four, five, six,
seven, eight, nine,
ten giant bags of garbage.

Captain Ned smiled. "Now, how about a ride on the *Sea Fan*?"

"Yo-ho!" shouted Jake.

Everyone followed Captain Ned to the dock. The waves whooshed as he steered his boat out to sea.

"Can we clean out here, too?" asked Natalie.

Mr. Tate gave them each a long pole with a net on the end.
As the class pulled trash from the water, dolphins leapt nearby.

"This sea is better now," said Captain Ned.

A spray of water misted the boat.

"That feels good! Thank you, Sea," said Amy.

"Yo-ho!" said Eli.

The splash on oceans and seas

When you walk across a beach or splash in the surf, you've stepped into the incredible world of water that covers three-quarters of our earth. This "world ocean," as scientists call it, is continuous, with five major regions: the Atlantic, Pacific, Indian, Arctic, and Southern (or Antarctic). Seas, such as the Mediterranean, are smaller bodies of water. They are connected to oceans, but mainly surrounded by land. (The word "sea" is commonly used as a synonym for "ocean.")

From the tiny, drifting phytoplankton (fahy-tuh-PLANGK-tuhn) plants smaller than the head of a pin to the massive blue whale, the oceans and seas contain hundreds of thousands of species of fish, animals, and plants. Marine scientists continue to discover hundreds of new species every year.

The world's climate and weather rely on the oceans and seas to move water through the atmosphere in a never-ending sequence known as the *water cycle*. Rain falls and snow melts into rivers and streams, which eventually flow into the oceans. The sun warms the water's surface into vapor, which rises into the sky. There it cools and forms clouds that will rain or snow, and continue the cycle of water. The oceans and seas also moderate our climate, so our world isn't too hot or too cold.

Humans depend on food from all kinds of fish and even seaweed and kelp. Overfishing and trawling, or dragging the ocean floor with nets, threaten to wipe out some species of fish such as Chilean sea bass. Other natural resources we use from our oceans and seas include salt, sand, gravel, crude oil, and minerals such as manganese, copper, nickel, iron, and cobalt. Several medicines for treating diseases, including cancer, are made from underwater plants and creatures like the sponge.

Most important, oceans and seas help make our air breathable. One teaspoon of seawater can hold millions of phytoplankton. Like trees and plants on land, phytoplankton use sunlight, carbon dioxide (CO_2), and water in a process called *photosynthesis* (foh-tuh-SIN-thuh-sis) to produce oxygen. Without oxygen, humans and animals could not exist on Earth. Phytoplankton also help soak up excess CO_2 created when we burn coal to produce electricity and use gasoline to power our cars. Too much CO_2 pollutes our air and damages delicate underwater ecosystems such as coral.

Another major threat to our oceans and seas is oil spills from drilling accidents and damaged, leaking tankers. These human-made environmental disasters have caused the death of hundreds of thousands of seabirds and animals, and continue to affect the habitat where the spills occurred. Dumping of raw sewage and chemicals also pollutes our oceans and seas and can harm human health.

The plastic bags, water bottles, soda cans, and other trash washed into our oceans and seas also harm marine life. Birds, fish, seals, and turtles have become entangled in or died from eating floating plastics. The Great Pacific Garbage Patch is a floating mass of trash, called *marine debris*, in the northern Pacific Ocean. It's the size of Rhode Island and keeps growing.

Everything in our natural world is connected. Even if you don't live near an ocean or sea, remember that your neighborhood creeks, streams, and rivers all flow into the world of water that covers most of our planet. Next time you visit a beach, splash in the waves. Breathe in the salty air. And remember how much seas count.

To Annette, Carolyn, Jody, Judith, Mona, Rachel, and Sheri. Critcasters count!—A.F.

To Will Sweeney.—S.S.

Special thanks to Dr. Thomas M. Grothues, The Institute of Marine and Coastal Sciences, Rutgers University.

Library of Congress Cataloging-in-Publication Data

Formento, Alison.
These seas count! / Alison Formento ; illustrated by Sarah Snow.
p. cm.
Summary: When Mr. Tate's class helps out on Beach Clean-Up Day, Captain Ned teaches the children the importance of the sea and the impact of not keeping it clean.
ISBN 978-0-8075-7871-1
(1. Oceans—Fiction. 2. Environmental protection—Fiction. 3. Water—Pollution—Fiction. 4. School field trips—Fiction. 5. Counting.) I. Snow, Sarah, ill. II. Title.
PZ7.F6764Tgs 2013
(E)—dc23
2012026187

Text copyright © 2013 by Alison Formento.
Illustrations copyright © 2013 by Sarah Snow.
Published in 2013 by Albert Whitman & Company.
ISBN 978-0-8075-7871-1

The design is by Nick Tiemersma.

For more information about Albert Whitman & Company, visit our web site at www.albertwhitman.com.

Also by Alison Formento
and Sarah Snow

SELECTED BIBLIOGRAPHY
Author correspondence and interviews with Dr. Thomas M. Grothues, Rutgers University.

Danson, Ted, and Michael D'Orso. *Oceana: Our Endangered Oceans and What We Can Do to Save Them.* Emmaus, PA: Rodale Books, 2011.

Earle, Sylvia A. *The World Is Blue: How Our Fate and the Ocean's Are One.* Des Moines, IA: National Geographic, 2010.

Levete, Sarah. *Destroying the Oceans.* New York, NY: Crabtree Publishing, 2010.

Moore, Captain Charles, with Cassandra Phillips. *Plastic Ocean: How a Sea Captain's Chance Discovery Launched a Determined Quest to Save the Oceans.* New York, NY: Avery, 2011.

Perretta, Dr. John. *Guide to the Oceans.* Richmond Hill, Ontario, Canada: Firefly Books, 2004.

Rose, Paul, and Anne Laking. *Oceans: Exploring the Hidden Depths of the Underwater World.* Berkeley, CA: University of California Press, 2008.

WEB LINKS
National Oceanic and Atmospheric Administration:
   www.noaa.gov
   www.oceanexplorer.noaa.gov
   www.fishwatch.gov
www.ocean.si.edu
www.nrdc.org/oceans/default.asp